Contemporary Chinese Poetry
in English Translation Series

Zang Di
Selected Poems

Translated by Fan Jinghua（得一忘二）

教育部人文社会科学重点研究基地
安徽师范大学中国诗学研究中心 组编
Chinese Poetry Research Center of Anhui Normal University

杨四平 主编　　上海文化出版社

当代汉诗英译丛书

臧棣诗歌英译选

[新加坡] 得一忘二 译

CONTENTS

目录

HANGING HIGH

J'ai décidé d'être tout le monde
—Arthur Rimbaud

Even a body so clear as to be shiny
cannot help but be convinced; it rises up
and floats towards a brimful self-circle;

At the juncture of track-merger, its brilliance has
become so dense that, for every 8,000 miles,
a red cloud takes away a tiger's roar or a leaning tower;

It shines, and this implies it has always
opposed hollowness and yearned for a symmetry
that is not invalidated by the world's evils;

Something is cruelly cold, but it is not
the easiness of our realization that we have already
reached the end of humanity;

高悬

> 我决定成为每个人
> —— 阿尔蒂尔·兰波

澄明到皎洁的通体
也不得不服气；它升起来，
飘向一个充盈的自圆；

并轨之际，清辉已绵密到
每隔八千里，就有一朵彤云
刚刚没收过虎啸或斜塔；

而照耀本身意味着
它始终反对空心，并渴望那个对称
并没有因人世的险恶而失效；

冷酷的，并不是我们
很容易就意识到我们
已走到了人类的尽头；

Now tightening, now relaxing,
it arranges our gaze as if there are
all the secrets in human pride;

It had long tested out that darkness is like a coarse grindstone
with its sharp consequence:
besides you, the heart does not need any other miracles.

时而收紧，时而放松
它布置我们的目光就好像
人的骄傲里有全部的秘密；

它早已试出黑暗像粗粝的磨刀石，
以及它的锋利的后果：
除了你，心并不需要别的奇迹。

1996.6

1998.7

EXTRAORDINARY GIFTS

Diamonds explode, roses are sharp,

The bright moon casts a yellow hue on the bird's nest,

We arrive at each other in our strangeness;

We are ambivalently affectionate as a sister and younger brother

Seeing ourselves as better people than an angel on the cliff;

I've brought along a spear but it is like Shakespeare

And cannot possibly have only one meaning; cosmetic darkness

Is unfathomable because of the allegory of the cave, while

We appear to have found the only entrance; the wuthering wind

Presses my hand tightly on the dorsal fin of the great white shark;

At least half of divinity should come from

Smoothness of this moment. Tenderness has become too shallow,

And only the inner brilliance can now illuminate

The sounds of nature as echoes, while human memory

Could never have reached this degree

Of profundity: to accept me is to shake me;

Violent ups and downs, until the breath of the sea

Returns the swans on our bodies

To the wings of the dawn.

非常礼物

钻石爆炸，玫瑰锋利，
皎洁的月亮令鸟巢发黄，
我们在彼此的陌生中抵达彼此；
我们矛盾于我们是深情的姐弟，
比悬崖边的天使更像好人；
我带来了长矛，但这就好像莎士比亚
不可能只有一个意思；宇宙的黑暗
因为一个洞穴的隐喻而
深不可测，我们仿佛找到了
那唯一的入口；呼啸的风
将我的手死死按在大白鲨的背鳍上；
一半的神性至少应出自
此时的光滑。温柔已经太浅，
所以，才有内部的灿烂
照亮过天籁即回声；人的记忆
原本不可能深远到
这一步：接纳我即颠簸我；
剧烈的起伏，直到大海的呼吸
将我们身上的天鹅
重新递还给黎明的翅膀。

1998.4

IF IT IS BRONZE
— AFTER PAUL VALÉRY

The lance of youth will be buried,

The song of the shadow will find mysterious comfort

From the swaying grass, until you have mastered

How to turn courage into inspiration

And to face the next round of more suspicious temptation—

All the detours are nothing but illusions;

The sense of heaviness will be replaced by the contradictions

Of the soil, the boundless darkness will extend itself

Into a gift more tranquil than death,

Waiting for you to receive. Free of charge, but still

It is worth asking: who are you? If a wrong mirror

Is used in front of you, who will I be then?

If after the size is distinguished, according to logic,

There is still a distant love, and while not transparent,

It contains damp clues…

The trumpet will rust, and the beautiful pattern

Will put another pair of strange eyes on test,

Until the sound of the piano brews a more charming form,

To break through time's imprisonment of us.

如果是青铜
——仿保尔·瓦雷里

青春的长矛将会被埋没，
影子之歌将会从摇晃的草叶上
找到神秘的安慰，直到你
已精通将勇敢变成灵感，
去面对下一轮更可疑的试探——
所有的迷途都不过是假象；
沉重感将被泥土的矛盾替代，
无边的黑暗，会把它自己扩展成
一件比死亡还平静的礼物，
等待你去领取。免费，但不妨
问一问：你是谁？如果用错了镜子，
在你面前，我又会是谁？
如果区分了大小之后，逻辑中
依然存在着遥远的爱，不透明
却包含着湿漉漉的线索……
小号将生锈，美丽的图案
将考验另一双陌生的眼睛，
直到琴声酝酿出更迷人的身体，
去突破时间对我们的禁锢。

1995.9
1998.12

THE PORE

To show how it exists,

it has also dug

a tiny hole in you

that cannot be tinier. Very beautiful

and so snuggly tight

that you rarely think of it.

Until you return to dust,

it is not to be absent for an instant;

it once concealed a kind of gentleness,

revealing that wild chrysanthemums also

grow out of the pores of the earth.

At any time, when the rabbits on you

startle and begin to jump,

or when a wild horse breaks free

and tears open a rift on you,

it will expand vigorously, discharging

the foul sweat through secret channels

into your naked skin,

making you as real as a dog in a downpour

running toward a pavilion.

毛孔

为了表明它是如何存在的，
它在你身上也挖了
一个小得不能
再小的孔眼。非常美，
而且又贴得这么紧，
你却很少想起它。
在你重新归入尘土之前，
它不可须臾或缺；
它隐藏过一种温柔，
就好像野菊花也是
从大地的毛孔中长出的。
任何时候，只要你身上的
兔子开始惊窜，跳跃，
或者一匹脱缰的野马
从你身上撕开了一道裂口时
它就会加紧扩张，
从一个个秘密渠道将那些臭汗
排放到你的赤裸中，
令你真实得就像暴雨中
有一条狗正朝凉亭跑去。

1998.8
1999.5

HOWL

Only when its echo is incorporated
into a pure contrast, quieter
than the night, will it quiver lightly with the abyss
on the hemp rope.

A bird can expose a vertex of darkness
merely with its cry;
resonance is perhaps a prelude,
but it will not spread far.

Visibility is low. On the slope,
it appears there is a pack of desert wolves
who have exhausted all their loneliness in the vastness
through dancing; until under the flickering starlight,

The earth presents itself as the best dance partner.
In a distant gaze, their long howls
have melted the sharpness of knife-like eyes,
and even heated up mysterious beliefs;

Thus, after hammering, darker than pitch black,
all the cages are left to with only one door open inward;
the path untraveled yet is suspended,
like a dragging aria suffocating you in the air.

长啸

只有将它的回音
纳入一种纯粹的对比，
比黑夜更沉寂的，才会和深渊一起
在麻绳上轻轻抖动。

一只鸟用它的叫声
就能暴露黑暗中的一个顶点；
共鸣或许就是序曲，
但不会传播得很远。

能见度很低。坡地上，
像是有一群荒原狼
在苍茫中把所有的孤独
都跳累了；直到闪烁的星光下，

大地原来是最好的舞伴。
遥远的直视中，它们的长啸
熔化过刀子一般的眼神，
甚至加热过神秘的信念；

如此，锤击之后，比漆黑更幽暗的，
所有的笼子都只剩下一扇朝里敞开的门；
未走过的道路，悬浮着，
像一个拖腔将你憋在空气的稀薄中。

1992.6
1998.10

RETURN FROM CLOUD PLAT FROM MOUNTAIN

Many butterflies on the way up the mountain.

The summer scenery, with its flaunting little flowery skirts,

is not just steep and daunting;

its fascinating details, ephemeral incarnations,

seem to have almost been taken up by the tiny

butterfly wings. After removing their masks,

they are most likely lighter natives.

To drive the mist, you don't have to

ride the clouds. Yes, what is ephemeral

may well be used as an elastic band.

To take it as a potential dance partner,

the first thing you should do is to clarify:

the difference between one passer-by and another

has become so great that the devil does not always

come from hell. The current situation is a bit entangled

with the angels being overly reliant on

that good people must not be too foolish.

Then, does giving subjectivity a pair of beautiful wings

instantly invalidate all the previous applications?

For the remaining steps, you don't even have to

declare: the butterfly is my premise.

云台山归来

上山时，蝴蝶很多。
小花裙招摇夏日的景色
不止是很陡峭；
迷人的局部，缥缈的化身，
看样子都快要被蝴蝶小小的翅膀
分配完了。面具摘下后，
它们最有可能是
更轻盈的土著。不必腾云，
你也可以驾雾。没错，
缥缈作为松紧带，
也很好用。而作为潜在的
舞伴，你首先要做的是
澄清：过客和过客之间
差别已大到魔鬼并不总是
来自地狱。目前的情况
有点纠缠于天使
太依赖好人不能太笨。
那么，给主体性也插上
一对美丽的翅膀
是否意味着，过去的所有申请
都可以被直接作废。
剩下的步骤，你甚至都
不必声称：蝴蝶是我的前提。

2001.9

NIGHT FREIGHT TRUCKS

Thunderous as vigilante justice.
The world's tremors shake a metallic switch
into your mind; the more you dredge,
the closer the spinning of the wheels
is to an insane gamble;
all signs indicate that the high beam from the headlights
becomes sharper than fangs.

The midnight door, the door of silence, the door of nature,
the door of the valley, the door of the season, the door of time,
the door of destiny, and the door of happiness that has just
flashed by your mind are all knocked down,
crushed and swept into the roar of machinery.
New greetings are pertinacious when facing
the cosmetic nasal sound that is more than a clang.

夜行货车

轰响如同私刑。
世界的摇晃将一个金属开关
震落到你的脑海中；
越打捞，车轮的旋转
越接近疯狂的赌注；
种种迹象显示，远光灯射出的光柱
已比獠牙还尖利。

午夜之门，静寂之门，自然之门，
山谷之门，季节之门，时间之门，
命运之门，以及你刚刚想到的
幸福之门，全都被撞飞；
被碾压，被卷入机械的吼叫；
新的问候语执拗于
宇宙的鼻音岂止很哐当。

Realizing that you can no longer fall asleep,
you get up from the bed,
and the beautiful beetle you've carefully fed for years
refuses to further metamorphose.
In the stalemate of the detours, you are compelled
to push open the rusty window of the small inn.

As expected, the highway and the room are too close together;
but staying overnight in the countryside, shouldn't it be natural
for the sacred negligence to have a different meaning?
After the curse, the new focus gradually shifts
to the moonlight, under which the country road
winds, like a freshly fired cannon barrel,
glowing fuzzily in the breath of ghosts.

意识到再也无法入睡后，
你从床上爬起来，
那只精心喂养了多年的
漂亮的大甲虫居然拒绝
进一步的变形；
僵持的迂回中，你只好推开
小旅店锈迹斑斑的窗户。

果然，公路和房间挨得太近了；
但夜宿乡野，神圣的疏忽
不是应该天然就另有含义吗？
诅咒之后，新的看点渐渐集中于
月光下，蜿蜒的乡间公路
犹如刚刚发射过炮弹的
炮膛，幽亮在幽灵的呼吸中。

2001.8
2002.6

BY THE ROAD THROUGH SOUTHERN ANHUI

As the wheels turn,
the valley stretches on for several hours
until the enormous silence suddenly
settles beneath the ancient shade of camphor trees
like a ball coming to rest.

If one is not too demanding,
it seems that a secret source has already been discovered.
The shade is ancient, yet the silence is fresh.
With every breath, the wick of the lantern
Is made to sway lightly.

On the half-slope, a row of homerun inns crouches
like yellow cows in a sweet potato field in a magnifying glass.
All the orders are suggesting
That after the nightfall there will be a sleep
to rival the full moon night in the Genesis.

取道皖南

随着车轮的转动，
山谷已经绵延了好几个小时，
直至巨大的寂静突然像
一个再滚不动的球，触靠在
樟树古老的荫影中。

不那么挑剔的话，
一个秘密的源头仿佛已经被找到。
荫影很古老，寂静却很新鲜。
每一阵呼吸，都能让
提灯的灯芯轻轻摇曳。

半坡上，一排民宿像放大镜里
半蹲在红薯地里的黄牛。
所有的秩序都在暗示
入夜后将会有一个睡眠
足以媲美创世纪的月圆之夜。

2001.6

BITTER RAIN

The message, although faint, has an unmistakable effect,
not to be misconstrued; the newly grown leaves,
of all sizes, sway and stagger
under the remote bombardment of raindrops.

Such is the sight a few days after the Awakening of Insects
when the first bitter rain of your life rustles down,
and you find yourself squatting
on a secluded stone slab in Yannan Garden, feeding cats.

Two piebald cats don't shy away at a cautious distance,
but act quite affably, snuggling around
and rubbing against your ankles, as if you emit a scent
that you yourself can never smell.

苦雨

虽然微弱但传递的
效果不会被误解，刚刚长成的
大大小小的绿叶踉跄着，
承受着雨珠的远程击打。

就这样，惊蛰刚过没几天，
人生中的第一场苦雨
簌簌落下时，你正蹲在
燕南园僻静的石板上喂猫；

两只花猫不仅不认生，
还很亲人，围着你的脚踝
蹭来蹭去，就好像你身上
有你永远都嗅不出的某种气息。

This small gesture reflects a hint
too obvious to miss, and inspires,
like a live example: you have also smelt
a certain scent unique to the spring rain.

This bitter rain that falls at the foot of Yan Mountains
contains a diagnosis of fate;
the green leaves washed by the rain
will be part of the healing.

If you have the desire to chew, be bolder —
let the sense of reality show its gnawed bark,
and let the love and death that swirl around you
be stirred more violently by the pitter-pattering rain.

这小动作折射出的暗示
太明显，以至于启发
就像现场举例，你也嗅出了
只属于春雨的某种气息。

下在燕山脚下的，这苦雨，
包含对命运的诊断；
被雨水洗刷过的绿叶
将是治愈的一部分；

想咀嚼的话，就再大胆点——
让现实性露出被啃过的树皮，
让围绕着你的爱与死
被这淅沥的水搅拌得再狠一点。

1988.4
1993.4

ABYSS DAY

Falling from the clouds, falling from a horse's back,
falling from a snow-covered bridge,
falling from a gentle embrace...
Different ways of falling should have pierced
through all sorts of loopholes in history,
but strangely enough, no one
sitting around the bonfire remembered
how exactly he had fallen. The sense of space
becomes increasingly focused only on
one place that could barely be called the bottom.
Although rockworks outnumber fake trees,
there is no intentional ignorance of fake flowers.
Dreams are also a bottom, but since they
correspond to the ephemeral reality, they are
drastically different from the here and now.
What is most unfathomable is not
that there is no real death in the abyss
but that no matter how you look at it, the butterfly
always looks perfectly well. When they lift
their clothes to examine each other, the healed scars
are more beautiful marks than wounds. And some scars
look almost exactly like butterflies.

深渊日

从云端坠落，从马背坠落，
从白雪覆盖的桥上坠落，
从温柔的怀抱坠落……
不同方式的坠落，应该击穿过
各种各样的历史的漏洞，
但是很奇怪，围坐在火堆旁，
竟然没有一个人记得
他是如何坠落的。空间感
越来越集中于只有
一个地方勉强可以叫做底部。
就连假山多于假树，
也谈不上有意忽略过假花。
梦，也是一个底部，
但因为对应于缥缈的现实，
所以，不同于此时此刻。
最深不可测的，还不是
深渊里没有真正的死，
而是蝴蝶，怎么看上去
一点事也没有。把衣服掀起来，
互相察看时，愈合的划痕
与其说是伤疤，不如是
美丽的记号。而且有些疤痕
看起来，几乎和蝴蝶一模一样。

1998.6
1999.1

FLYING DAY

The weather forecast is not accurate;

the cloudy sky has not turned timely into a clear one

with a rainbow bowing. At the far end of the horizon,

the hazy shroud not only lowers the skyline

but also shortens the view,

yet one can still feel that the air around

has been stirred up by invisible wings;

it is obvious that the world's emotions

are not just combed by the wind.

Birds fly over the treetops,

the shadow of fate sways lightly.

The sense of suspension feels the greenness

that you are aware of whether you have ever favored furry ovals.

It is time now, please do not evade

the possibility—

that birds have flown past you; then, you find yourself

clearly in some kind of charming sway

that you have never experienced before.

飞翔日

天气预报并不准确，
多云并未及时转向有彩虹
鞠躬的晴朗。视线尽头，
灰蒙蒙的笼罩感，不仅压低了
天际线，也缩短了远眺；
但还是能感觉到，四周的空气
已被无形的翅膀煽动起来；
很明显，世界的情绪
不仅仅只是经过了风的梳理。

鸟飞过树梢，
命运的影子轻轻晃动。
悬空感碧绿于你很清楚
你有没有偏爱过毛茸茸的椭圆形。
是时候了，请不要回避
是否存在过那种可能性 ——
鸟掠过你；接着，你发现你
已明显处于过去从未经历过的
某种迷人的晃动之中。

1998.5
1999.2

PRIMAL BLOSSOM
— AFTER PETER HUCHEL

A chance encounter alone
cannot suffice to bring about its miracle.

If you seek delicacy, go elsewhere to brawl.
If you crave coquetry, try to find a shortcut
outside reality.

As for this, humanity is but a fortuitous premise.
Yet it does not rely on
when you can eventually break free from the mystery of fate.

The flavor of seasons is already
quite delicate; and, to add on this,
the musical strings of time are often unreliable,
what can you do if you are not
out of you-in-me?

初花
——仿彼得·胡赫尔

唯一的相遇，还不足以
成就它的奇迹。

喜欢娇嫩，请去别处撒野。
陶醉妖艳，请另辟现实中
还有没有捷径。

对于它，人不过太是偶然的前提。
它却不依赖于你何时
才能从命运之谜中挣脱出来。

季节的味道本来
就已非常娇气；再加上
时间的琴弦又常常不那么争气，
万一你并不来自
你中有我，怎么办？

Inside the common ground, secrets
exist in the profound silence
that contradicts the silent body.

The sole hope lies in that you may sense ahead of time
the urgency of time's increasing rarefication;
and the only witness,
if unavoidable, has to be absolutely accurate—

What this poem can guarantee, is merely
something intangible, and it can feel
your hand touching it, as well as
the touch's end
that is akin to the end of the universe.

Note: Peter Huchel (1903-1981) was a German poet.

共同之处，秘密存在于
深刻的安静矛盾于
安静的身体。

唯一的希望，你有可能会提前
紧迫于时间越来越稀薄；
以及那唯一的见证
如果不得不涉及必须绝对准确 ——

这首诗能保证的，也只是
无形，它却能感觉到你的手
对它的触摸，以及
那触摸的尽头
几近无异于宇宙的尽头。

1998.4
1999.7

注：彼得·胡赫尔（Peter Huchel，1903—1981），德国诗人。

THE BEAUTY OF THE WORLD

Different seasons will have
different contours. The choice of feathers
can be drastically different
from that of petals. Don't think that
the stirs of secrets will easily spare you
only because you do not have visible feathers.
The fissures are small, but the vortex of beauty
won't mind if your breath seems a bit short.
The arrangement of seasons should be attributed
to an underpinning. Being born in spring differs
from being born in autumn, and it means that
when men and women fall in love, the meeting place
will have already been redressed by the will of heaven.
Exquisite petals may be eye-catching,
but they are just a gentle shape
needed for bees to fulfill their contract;
undoubtedly, there are beautiful butterflies
in the shades of the testers too.
The moment you are taken away from your ancient body,

世界的美

从云端坠落，从马背坠落，
不同的季节会有
不同的轮廓。羽毛的选择
和花瓣的选择会有
很大的差别。不要以为
你身上没有明显的羽毛，
秘密的煽动就会轻易放过你。
缝隙很小，但美的旋涡
不会嫌弃你的呼吸是否有点急促。
季节的安排应归结为
一次兜底。诞生在春天
和出生在秋天，意味着
男人和女人相恋时，汇合的地点
早已被天意纠正过。
娇美的花瓣很醒目，但也不过是
对蜜蜂履行契约时
需要一个温柔的形状；
当然，测试者的身影中
也不乏美丽的蝴蝶。
你被带离古老的身体；

the wandering begins, and a memory will take shape

when the resurrected one tries in his unending gaze

to conclude the boundary of the soul

at the end of the cries of cranes. Springtime scenery

is charming indeed, but I prefer the Nature in autumn.

The leaves are golden and will prepare

the paint for memory; if you want to practice

perfect handstands, the burning twilight

will yield the biggest loophole in the world.

In the familiar smell, a small harvest

will be able to make you walk out of any enclosed cave.

漫游开始，一个记忆因而成形于
复活者试图在无尽的眺望中
将灵魂的边界总结在
鹤唳的尽头。春天的景象
确实很迷人，但我更偏爱
秋天的大自然。金黄的落叶
已准备好记忆的颜料；
想练习完美的倒立，燃烧的黄昏
就是最大的世界的漏洞。
熟悉的味道中，一次小小的丰收，
就能令你走出封闭的洞穴。

1999.7

2002.5

THE CONTESTED WORLD

Sometimes, a chestnut tree growing in heaven

And a pine tree growing in hell

Do not look very different from afar,

But the problem is, a crow may not

See it that way; have you noticed that

Whenever and wherever chance encounters

Occur, there is always a pair of captivating eyes

That will leave a deep impression on us;

The gaze of a crow, compared with yours,

Is always more attentive, more vigilant.

Even when in love, your gaze is deeply engrossed,

So unabashed that it appears to bash the bones,

But still cannot compare to the gaze of a crow

Staring intently at a pinenut in a glass jar.

The bleakness of the world is a theatrical show.

The valley in winter, with few human traces,

Presents an incomparable mise-en-scène.

世界的较量

有时，一棵长在天堂的栗子树
和一棵长在地狱的松树，
远远看去，区别不是很大。
但问题是，一只乌鸦
很可能不这么看；不知你
注意到没有：任何时候，任何地方，
只要涉及不期而遇，就有一对
迷人的眼神令我们印象深刻；
乌鸦的眼神永远都比
你的眼神显得更专注，更机敏。
即便恋爱时，你的眼神
已非常专注，露骨到近乎刻骨，
但仍然没法和乌鸦盯着
玻璃瓶里的松仁时的眼神相比。
世界的荒凉是一出戏。
入冬后的山谷，人迹稀少，
效果堪比最好的舞台。

The crow flies down from a tree, approaches you,

As if it intuitively realizes that humans,

Being merely passers-by, wherever they go,

Will always leave some rubbish behind them—

The smell is, like the mixture of angels and demons,

Difficult to tell from each other once it enters the air.

What the devil looks like, the crow can never tell.

The disadvantage does not stop here,

Crows are born black, even darker

Than the darkest blindfold by ten thousand times;

But once reality responds to this differently from

What the truth does: countless black shadows flash by,

And your eyes will be polished by the crows;

As if whether you are an angel or not,

The crows nearby have always taken a crucial step.

乌鸦从树上飞下，靠近你，
就好像在它的直觉里，
人，这种过客，无论走到哪儿，
身上总会留下点垃圾——
味道有点像天使和魔鬼
一旦混入空气就很难区分。
魔鬼长什么样，乌鸦无法给出答案。
不利的一面不止于此，
乌鸦长得很黑，比最黑的
蒙眼布还要黑上一万倍；
而真实一旦作出不同于
真相的反应：无数的黑影闪过，
你的眼神反而会被乌鸦擦亮；
就好像你是不是天使，
靠近的乌鸦，已迈出了关键的一步。

1998.3
1999.6

BUTTONS OF TIME

At dawn, they are dazed in the reflections of the morning glow.
At dusk, they are quieted by the contrast of the fiery clouds.

How mysterious it is to distinguish! A sensitive finch
Won't waste on them the time that belongs to squirrels.

So small is the aperture that when it is applied to impossible euphemisms,
The gazer will have already transcended the spying of the world.

After the swapping of roles, I unfasten the buttons of time,
Like pulverizing the rock within a rock.

It opens so suddenly that there must be
Another reason for subtle acceptance.

At least, the breath of love appears to be
A stolen golden apple being reignited at its fuse.

This is how I introduce myself: if these buttons remain
Fastened, the labyrinth will be more depraved than hell.

时间的扣子

早晨，它们迷乱于霞光的反射。
傍晚，它们安静于火烧云的反衬。

鉴别多么神秘。敏感的雀鸟
不会在它们身上浪费属于松鼠的时间。

缝隙很小，用于不可能的委婉，
凝视者已脱胎于世界的窥视。

角色互换后，我解开时间的扣子，
像粉碎岩石里的岩石。

敞开很突然，所以，微妙的接纳
必须另有一个原因。

至少看上去，爱的呼吸即偷走的
金苹果被重新点燃了引信。

我这样介绍我自己：这些扣子
再不解开的话，迷宫会比地狱更堕落。

1996.9
1997.2

PURPLE RAINCOAT

Che nascerà dopo mill' anni

—*Francesco Petrarch*

You were drawn into its magic, though
You wore it only once; you vanished inside it
Without a trace, like the conspicuous
Vanishing of a showgirl from the stage.
There is no need to smooth those folds,
As it's the loneliest of the props.
If there is any chance to come back
To that rainy day, I might wake up suddenly—
Both mobile and cruising,
It looks like a shark's dorsal fin,
A not-so-great friendship mismatched.

紫色雨衣

> ……诞生还需要一千年
> —— 彼特拉克

你只穿过一次，
它就把你带进了它的魔术；
如同大变活人一样，
你在它里面阒然消失了。
无需将那些皱褶抹平，
它也是最孤独的道具。
如果还有机会回到
那个雨天，或许会猛醒——
既是移动也是游弋，
它看上去像鲨鱼的背鳍，
还算不上伟大的友谊已错位。

Hidden choices have been touched,
Its color tinged onto any background
Will appear emotional. A purple sun
May be more common than purple moons,
Therefore, when it is overcast, the falling
Purple rain will remind you that
You have misunderstood we are colorblind.
Besides, the ups and downs of fate will inevitably
Affect the wear and tear that the memory of life
Inserts on it. For such an old thing,
Wherever it hangs is a site awaiting an excavation;
When it hangs behind the door,
Half the universe can no longer be opened.

隐秘的选择已被触及，
它的颜色放到任何背景中
都会显得很情绪。紫太阳
比紫月亮更常见，所以
天阴沉下来时，飘落的紫雨
会启发你误解过
我们究竟有没有色盲。
此外，命运的沉浮
难免会影响到人生的记忆
对它的磨损。一件旧物，
它挂在哪里，哪里就像现场
等待着一次发掘；它挂在门后，
半个宇宙就再也无法打开。

1997.5
1999.2

A STUDY OF GOLDEN CICADAS

The fact is, no one has ever seen a golden cicada,

let alone a magical shell

Like a widget overflowing with gold dust

That follows the general orientation of bones

And slowly breaks away. In reality,

More often than not, the shadow is caused by the fact

That every statue enjoys swaying with the wind.

The lesson from green willow's hospitality

Is sufficient to support such a conclusion:

A real cicada needs none of the flippant

Gold dust; no matter how splendid

The paint looks, it is unnecessary.

A great cicada will need even less superficial

Adornment. In fact, those who desire

To slough off the shell are all your kind:

Undefined in bondages and frivolous in shortcuts.

It is too difficult to trace the source back to

Transparent wings. Naturally, once you realize

You can reduce some weight, you can ask

A timely question: Do you really

Have ever had a kind like that?

金蝉学

其实，没有人见过金蝉；
更遑论一个神奇的壳
就像流溢着金粉的小品一样
被它顺着骨骼的走势
缓缓脱离。现实中，
更多的是，影子源于
每个雕像都喜欢随风晃动。
领教过柳绿的盛情，
足以得出这样的结论：
一只真正的蝉其实
不需要那些轻浮的金粉；
漆得再好看，也不需要。
一只伟大的蝉，就更不需要
那些外在的矫饰。渴望脱壳的，
其实是你的同类：既暧昧于
束缚，也轻浮于捷径。
想要溯源到透明的翅膀，太难了。
当然，一旦意识到可以减轻
某些重量时，你的确可以
及时反问：你真的
有过那样的同类吗？

1998.7
1999.2

FIRE DANCE

When the distinction between love and death
Comes across a rebounding rope, it may
Sometimes trigger the memory of fire dance.
Many fragments, and most of them
Have already been bleached by rain;
The rust-stained necklaces dug from the soil,
Even if well preserved, can no longer
Remember the golden glimmers of clues
That were once shown on their bodies.
Exclamations go up and down, and pigeons
Will carry them into the circling of the morning.
The melody is quite natural, although unrefined.
Invisible batons can feel in the pigeons' circlings
The seeds of time being continuously filtered into
Small cards of consciousness. A rough count
Will tell easily that the living people have hardly realized
They have ever been invited to a fire dance,
While the dead believe that they, by the arrangement
Of Death, must have already done the fire dance.
Otherwise, how can the transparency of hell and the lingering
Traces of the afterimage of life dance present themselves,
With such a stubborn silence, in this poem?

火舞

爱与死的区分遇到
反弹的绳子，有时会触发
有关火舞的回忆。
碎片很多，大部分
都已被雨水漂白，
从土里挖出的锈迹斑斑的项链，
即使保存得很完好，
也已不记得它们身上
曾有过的金光闪烁的线索。
起伏的感叹被鸽子带入
上午的盘旋。旋律很粗制，
但也很自然。看不见指挥棒，
可以感觉到时间的种子
在鸽子的盘旋里不断被过滤成
意识的小卡片。粗略编号后，
不难发现，活着的人
几乎从未意识到他们
曾被邀请去跳火舞；死去的人
则以为根据死神的安排，
他们肯定已跳过火舞。
否则，地狱的透明，以及从那里
透过来的，生命之舞的最后
一点影像的残留，又怎么可能
带着固执的沉默，呈现在这首诗中？

1997.5
1999.2

HOW TO EXPLAIN THE COLOR OF SHAME
— AFTER JOHN BERRYMAN

The colors of the soul, and the like,

seem to have moved the world's motives.

When you have compared, against the trajectory

of intangible things, too many non-colors,

it appears that several beautiful mushrooms have

suddenly sprouted in the corner of the universe;

whether or not they are edible depends

not on whether your judgement of toxicity and beauty

is accurate but rather on whether or not

your sense of shame is mixed with human sensitivity.

They are fabulously fleshy, so the reason

for their splendor should be more splendorous

than the mystery of the flesh. The weight of the earth

is too real, and mushrooms are like loosened nuts

of death, exposing the surface, implying

that you still have a chance to put yourself into use,

toward the same end, with the same force.

Therefore, when you realize that human shame

has color, finding it different from azure,

from orange-yellow, from rose red, and from the pitch-black

that death desperately recommends to you...

all signs indicate that you have not stopped evolving.

To borrow a TV catchphrase:

colored shame is unashamedly calcium-rich.

如何解释羞耻的颜色
——仿约翰·贝里曼

灵魂的颜色，诸如此类，
似乎牵动过世界的动机。
当你沿无形的事物的轨迹
比较过太多的无色，宇宙的角落
仿佛突然一下多出了好几朵
美丽的蘑菇；能不能食用
不在于你对毒性和美丽的判断
是否准确，而在于你的羞耻感
有没有混入人的敏感。
很肉感，所以，很鲜艳应该
另有一个比肉体的奥秘
更奇妙的解释。大地的沉重
太逼真，蘑菇像被拧松的
死亡的螺母，露出地表，暗示你
还有一次沿同样的方向，
以相同的劲道，使用自己的机会。
所以，当你觉察到人的羞耻
是有颜色的：不同于湛蓝，
不同于橙黄，不同于玫瑰红，
不同于死亡向你竭力推荐的漆黑……
种种迹象表明，你依然没有停止进化。
借用电视广告里的一句话：
有色的羞耻，很补钙。

1999.2

THE SOFTEST FRUIT

There is no choice. When you first

lay eyes on it, it had to be golden.

It would not allow any other image or form;

it would not allow itself to make

the same mistakes as you.

It had to mature as if it would never

beg for another chance.

Golden among the golden, unabashedly plump;

all the visible curves on it are so perfect

that the superhuman artistry was merely exquisite.

If your gaze did not contain that intuition,

it will plead that you have never seen it before.

Very soft, yet also very absolute.

It will not give you a chance to pinch it.

If you are overly soft, failing

to keep intact the boundary of your inner self,

it will fall prematurely from you,

falling into the awakening abyss, as if

death was once the softest fruit.

最柔软的果实

别无选择。在你第一次
看到它的时候，它必须是金黄的。
它不会放任其他的形象；
它不会允许自己再犯
和你一样的错误。它必须
成熟得就好像它绝不会祈求
再给它另外一个机会。
金黄中的金黄，饱满得毫无隐瞒；
在它身上，所有可见的弧度
都已完美到鬼斧也曾
十分玲珑。如果你的目光中
没有包含那个直觉，它会恳求
你从未见过它。非常柔软，
却也非常绝对。它不会给你捏它的机会。
如果你的柔软太过分，
辜负了内心作为一种界限，
它就会提前从你身上坠落，
坠向那觉醒的深渊，就好像
死亡也曾是最柔软的果实。

1994.9
1997.10

ASSOCIATION OF THE DEAD CORNERS OF MEMORY

On the way home, the birds' calls
pull the evening glow over the Yan Mountains
towards the almost motionless bare branches.
The change of sky light is visibly
more rushed than the summer, as if there were
a dark grey net that takes back the scenery
ten minutes earlier every day.
The paleness of the crescent moon matches perfectly
with the lonely stones that would rather
stay isolated in the cold symmetry
than participate in the morality of winter.

Splendid colors, scattered on the ground,
are more chaotic than the sighs of fate,
and they have never thought of dawdling away
an unexpected ending: these fallen leaves,
like sensitive brake pads, work on
the dead corners of memory,
making your shadow vaster than people's trances.
Don't underestimate the subtle differences.
If dead souls could resonate,
the best rhythm must exist in the falling leaves
gliding towards the floating ice's truth.

记忆的死角协会

归途中，鸟的叫声
将燕山的晚霞拽向
几乎静止不动的光秃枝条。
天光的变幻比夏天
明显要仓促，就好像有
一张灰黑的网，每天都会提前
十分钟，将风景收回去。
弯月的苍白，正符合
孤独的石头宁愿孤立在
冷酷的对称中，也不想
参与冬天的道德。

被吹落到地上，凌乱多于
命运的叹息，色彩的缤纷
尤其没想过要偷懒
一个结局：这些落叶
就像灵敏的刹车片一样，
作用于记忆的死角，
令你的影子多于人的恍惚。
不要小瞧这细微的分别。
如果死灵魂可以共鸣，
最好的节奏一定存在于
这些落叶正飘向浮冰的真理。

2003.12
2004.2

ASSOCIATION OF THE EXTRAORDINARY ORIGIN

The best memorial

Originates in the seasons of the heart.

At the heart of darkness, the heartbeat has perhaps already

Transformed. The background sound can be extremely faint,

But there must be a stone

To maintain an acute sense of suspension.

It also looks the same from afar.

The heart of darkness, the dark vortex

Has withdrawn to the starting point of consciousness;

When your heart beats faster, a stone is picking up speed

To spin in your tilted body

As if it is the drill of a comet.

It can surely stand up to close observation,

As if snows stick to the stone, shiny

Like the breath of stones at six thousand meters

Or higher, and they are also white —

So white that even the Death is forced to seek another disguise.

非常起源协会

最好的纪念
源自心灵的季候。
黑暗的中心，心跳或许已变形。
背景音可以弱到极点，
但必须有一块石头
保持着凌厉的悬空感。

从远处看，也是这样。
黑暗的中心，黑暗的旋涡
已退回到意识的起点；
心跳加速时，你倾斜的身体里
一块石头正飞速旋转
犹如彗星的钻头。

当然也经得起近观，
就好像石头上，附丽有积雪，
晶亮得像六千米以上
石头的呼吸，也是白色的——
白得令死神的屏息
也不得不另外寻找一种伪装。

2001.1

ASSOCIATION OF GLORIOSA DAISY

The disguise is artful, yet a black sun
Can still be seen captured in its flower heart
By the wax-yellow petals.
Even if you have misconceived a still storm,
It won't misconstrue you.
Then, a beehive-like exits is seen,
Rarely frequented in ordinary days;
But now, it suddenly opens you up;
And in ten seconds a decision must be made —
To choose a fantastic fragrance,
Risking to miss history or an eternal life;
To choose the filmy little wings
Means you will no longer need human memory.

金光菊协会

伪装很巧妙，但仍能看出
一颗黑太阳已被蜡黄的花瓣
俘虏在它的花心深处。
如果你误解过静止的风暴，
它也不会误解你。
接着，有一个类似蜂巢的出口，
平时几乎很少用到；
此刻，却突然将你打开；
十秒钟内必须做出一个决定——
选择奇异的花香，
你也许会错过历史或永生；
选择薄薄的小翅膀，
你就不再需要人的记忆。

2001.10
2004.3

ASSOCIATION OF ARIAS

A volcano-like eruption, but what drenches you
is a magnificent fountain. Before it is dried off,
sharp-edged tears had already cut open
a deep gash in your regret.
If there were scorching embers
raining down to bury you alive,
that's something for later. As this instant
is screwing down the moment, the dark valley
comes conveniently to replace the powered-off stage.
You can palpably feel your gorgeous body
turned on through secret pipelines.
Under such circumstances, adequacy is at best
overwhelming presence of water. It might come as a surprise,
but soon you will feel hypnotized
by surging emotions, more relaxed than in entrancement,
and you will need no excuse, as if
your personal expression has finally found a real
body, no longer confined by the good or evil of the role;
under such circumstances, it looks like
the scraps on the same contours are left by someone else.

咏叹调协会

火山般爆发，但将你淋湿的
是华丽的喷泉。不等到
及时烘干，锋利的泪滴
已将你的悔悟划开了
一道很深的口子。如果有烫人的
灰烬落下，并将你淹埋，
那也是后来的事。此刻
拧紧此时，幽黑的山谷
正好适合取代断电的舞台。
能明显感觉到，你的华丽的身体
已被秘密的管线接通。
这种情况下，只能说，充足很水量。
也许会有点吃惊，但很快
你就会觉得被喷涌的情感
催眠到比迷醉还放松，
而且无需借口另外的理由，
确实很像自我表现突然
找到了一个真身，不再受限于
角色的好坏；这种情况下
就好像等高的废品是别人留下的。

2005.5
2006.2

ASSOCIATION OF WITHERED GRASS

True, it is deep autumn, but still
there is a faint echo rebounding from
the exuberance of spring light, lingering
in its environs. If time turns back,
a few months ago, it was not someone else
but you who, capitalizing on the spoiled mood,
with an exaggerated tone, likened it
to a secluded beauty. But now, the once-smooth skin
has lost its moisture, and it withers and yellows
with a stubborn spirit of "seeing is believing;"
its slenderness and fragility, like two whip marks,
shape and deepen our gaze directed at it: compared
to the springtime, the withered yellow renders it
even more sensible and dignified than you.
It can be harmed by neither your hesitation
nor human melancholy. It even goes ahead of nature's morality
to modify the notion that its looks also deceive.

枯草协会

没错。现在虽然是深秋，
但依然有一个依稀的回音，
反弹自烂漫的春光，徘徊在
它的周围。时光回转，
几个月前，不是别人，正是你，
趁着被宠坏的兴致，
用夸张的口吻，将它类比成
偏僻的美人。而此刻，
曾经的肌肤已失去水分，
它枯黄在百闻不如一见的固执中；
细瘦和脆弱，如同两道鞭痕，
加深着它对我们投向
它的眼光的塑造：比起在春天，
正是那枯黄令它显得
比你还深明大义。你的犹豫，
抑或人的忧郁，都无从伤害到它。
它甚至会先于自然的道德
纠正它也属于不可貌相。

The cluttered sounds of wind rebound about

as if they have just passed through the scattered graves,

administrating the desolation of the universe.

The yellowness of the withered grass lies around, supine,

and decidedly it implicates a meaning

deeper than that of the world's taste. Obviously,

where it soars high, there is a mysterious illusion,

definitely not centering around you,

but taking it as the origin, which harvests

the qualities of life, the dance of the earth.

在它周围，凌乱的风声
像是刚刚穿过一片凌乱的坟墓，
整理着宇宙的荒凉。
斜卧在旁边，草木的枯黄
显然比世界的味道
更牵扯一个深意。很明显，
它矗立的地方，有一个
神秘的幻觉，全然不以你为中心，
而是以它为原点，收敛着
生命的品相，大地的舞姿。

2004.9
2006.2

ASSOCIATION OF TIDES

At this moment, it's best to use borrowed ears;

to avoid the world's silhouette getting

a little too dim, it's also necessary to stand erect,

as the door just been opened from inside

requires such a height. The sea breeze

has completely replaced the night wind,

and countless silver fish flip and tumble in the prelude

of Metamorphosis, almost striking out sparks

from the shimmering scales of the sea.

Surely, who you are is important; but

in front of the tide, who can tell

who you are seems more urgent.

Amid distracting thoughts, a calmness rises,

which is satisfying; removal distracting sounds requires

only a few fingerings on the moonlight strings,

which is leveraging; there is decidedly no need

to waste so much time so many preconditions as in the past.

Thus, the tide passing by your side can also be a precondition.

The aria of eternity can be simulated as if ancient advices

could be so mysterious that they do not need

the help of lips. You don't even need to argue

as the silver tide has taken off

another layer of clothing from your naked body.

潮汐协会

此时，耳朵最好是借来的。
为了避免世界的轮廓
有点幽暗，身体也最好直立，
因为刚刚从里面打开的
一扇门，需要这样的高度。
海风完全取代了夜风，
无数的银鱼翻滚在
变形记的序曲里，几乎要
将大海的鳞光擦出火花。
你是谁，固然很重要；
但在潮汐面前，谁能回答
你是谁，似乎更紧要。
杂念里有一个冷静，就已很好；
杂音的排除也只需拨弄几下
月光的琴弦，就可以将计就计；
完全没必要像过去那样，
大把的时间都浪费在了过多的前提上。
如此，潮汐掠过你的身边，
也可以是一个前提。
永恒的咏叹被模拟得就好像
古老的叮嘱完全可以神秘到
不必借助嘴唇。你甚至不想争辩，
银色的潮汐从你的裸身上
又脱下了一件衣服。

2001.12
2005.7

There is a stone somewhere in your body,

however, so far it remains a secret.

Even you yourself are not quite clear.

About this. Before the incident, your mind was described

As a piece of ore engraved with wild geese—

a few staggered scratches allured you

and made you obsessed with the simplicity in the simple,

as if a few more scratches would inspire you to spell out

a map of the mind, or wild geese's

out-of-print cries. You are heading west,

measuring your love with bare feet.

Upon waking up, wild weeds begin to power up

the bones that have folded to keep warm at night.

You are recovered as quickly as the dawn.

The way you walk is peculiar, as if

there is a group of elks galloping in front of you.

In this world, except for that stone,

nothing, it seems, is qualified to accuse you

for being so imprudent.

行吟诗人协会

你的身体里有一块石头，
不过，到目前为止，这是一个秘密。
甚至你自己都不十分清楚
这件事情。在此之前，你的心被描述成
一块上面刻了野鹅的矿石——
几条交错的划痕引诱你
迷恋简单中的不简单，就仿佛
再添上几道，你就会拼出
一张心灵的地图，或野鹅的
已经绝版的喊叫。你正向西而行，
用赤脚丈量你的爱。
一觉醒来，茂盛的荒草发电给
为取暖而折叠了一夜的骨头。
你恢复得像晨曦一样快。
你走起路来，样子很奇特，
就好像有一群麋鹿在你的前方颠跑着。
在这个世界上，除了那块石头，
似乎还没有一件东西有资格责怪你
为什么会如此大意。

2004.8

ASSOCIATION OF LOOPHOLES
— To JIANG HAO

Coldness, so prone to misunderstanding?
Coldness, what sort of fate is it? It's but
a steelyard scale that Time hands down.
Therefore, damned butterfly, since you've
lost my letter when overflying the last boundary,
you have to change back to a comet—
my reason for cringing at coldness is entirely different
from yours; it's like I can see distinctly
in my curses how I've fallen.

漏洞协会
　　——赠蒋浩

冷，就这么容易被误解吗？
冷，算什么命运？它不过是
时光递过来的一杆秤。
所以，该死的蝴蝶，既然你
在翻越最后一道界限时，弄丢了
我的信，你就必须再变回一颗彗星 ——
因为我怕冷的理由和你完全不同，
它有点像我在我的诅咒中
清晰地看见了我的堕落。

2013.10.25

A BOOK SERIES ON THE STUDY OF NOTHINGNESS

Forgive me, but I can only do this in absolute

darkness. With wings spread, I hover and glide,

and every juncture is dark enough to be unimaginable;

then, without deviation, I return to my marvelous foothold.

My mind, delved deep into the darkness, becomes highly focused.

I acquaint with the dark the way lions forgive atheism.

These grown-up lions are sleeping tight in your zodiac.

In my surroundings, only darkness is primal,

and only darkness can free itself from dark politics. It swallows

water-towers, apartment buildings, shabby bungalows,

small stony bridges, and the small lake at the end of the woods.

Darkness blurs all the boundaries. If you have not figured out

who I am, the absolute darkness will bring you an identity.

Forgive me, but there are things that have to be spelt out clearly:

without such darkness, there would be no cosmic happiness.

虚无学丛书

原谅我，我只能在绝对的黑暗中
才能做这件事情。展翅，盘旋，滑翔，
每个环节都黑暗得不难想象；
随后，准确地回到美妙的落脚点。
我的精神因深入黑暗而高度集中。
我领略黑暗，就像这些狮子原谅了无神论。
这些成年的狮子就睡在你的星座上。
在我的四周，只有这黑暗是原始的；
只有黑暗摆脱了黑暗的政治。黑暗吞没了水塔，
吞没了居民楼，吞没了小平房，
吞下了小石桥，咽下了林子尽头的小湖。
黑暗模糊了所有的界限。假如你不清楚我是谁，
绝对的黑暗会给你带去一个身份。
原谅我，有些事情必须表达得毫不含糊：
假如没有这黑暗，也就没有宇宙的幸福。

2008.7

A BOOK SERIES ON REVOLUTIONARY POETRY CANONS
— To WANG AO

This is the joy of existence: wild fires or wild grasses.

Interconnected, the spectacle lies in secret encouragement.

No need for explanation to run this dynamo, and who can ever bring fear!

Education is everywhere: wild vegetables will ripen

with a mere session of self-criticism. And wild fruits rot beside bushmeat,

diffusing a moral revolution. A stir of air

may present a beautiful space, to the extent

that wild men lie lower than wild flowers.

Their wildness humiliates nature. The end is but an illusion.

Do you still remember how we raced against time?

This was a wild pride, and you, mystery, had only

one friend and a half. That won't do, if it does not last forever—

this is a joy beyond the wits of gloomy ones.

This is an unorthodox way of chewing, and poetry sharpens our teeth.

革命的诗经丛书
——赠王敖

这是生存的欢乐：野火或者野草。
互相联系，壮观在秘密的激励中。
不解释就能发电，浑身怕过谁呵。
处处都是教育：自我批评一下，
野菜就熟了。而野果子腐烂在野味边上，
散发出道德的革命。一种气息
就能带来一个美妙的空间，甚至是，
野人躺得比野花还要低。
全都野得令自然羞愧。尽头只是假象。
你还记得我们怎样和时间赛跑吗？
这是野蛮的骄傲，神秘你只有
一个半朋友。不永恒，不行——
这是阴郁的人不能理解的欢乐。
这是不合规矩的咀嚼，诗在替我们磨牙。

2008.10

A BOOK SERIES ON THE MARVELOUS MINDS

This corner is yours now: no one comes from the end,

no one nearby passes by. Behind the grove,

lies the price of mystery. Games just over, no one has ever

imagined that a touchstone can be so lovely or thoughts can

be harder than basic instincts. There is so much sweat,

so watery that it cannot stand a touch. You want to know

how marvel is tempered? Not resorting to rituals means

examples are always ready. A dozen of black ants appear to

console life in detail: They crawl past fallen petals, and slowly

hold a peanut shell on their shoulders. From the tiny procession,

it should not be difficult to extract a black marching pace.

I am walking to a corner that is more abstract than human's fate.

I hope to help us figuring out: if, out of sheer carelessness,

we are turned to a marvel, what would you do? If we are turned to

a marvel before we are ready, do we have another chance?

美妙思想丛书

这角落现在是你的了：没有人从尽头走来，
也没有人从附近走过。灌木的背后
是一个神秘的代价。游戏刚刚结束，
没想到试金石会这么可爱。没想过
思想竟然比本能还要硬。流了这么多汗。
水汪汪的，一触即发。你不是想知道
美妙是怎么炼成的吗？不仪式，意味着
例子更现成。十几粒黑蚂蚁像是在安慰
人生的细节：它们绕过剥落的花瓣，
将花生壳缓缓抬起。从这小小的行进中，
提取一种黑色的步伐，应该不是什么难事。
我正走向比人的命运更抽象的角落。
我想帮助我们弄清楚：如果一不小心，
就被美妙了，你该怎么办？如果还没准备好，
就已经被美妙了，我们是否还有别的机会？

2008.10

A BOOK SERIES ON GOLDEN SECRETS

Head bent, I could only see this chrysanthemum,
a golden guide, small arms extending like tentacles of a mollusk.
You'd need a casual glance to see a picture of bright yellow petals.

Now my heartstring is fine like a broken string of an instrument.
Anything that's so well-raised must be wise in politics;
accordingly, the decorum of a plant holds occult messages of the cosmos.

Head up, I catch a glimpse of a person watering the flower.
She is not a gardener, and yet it appears she has a better way,
knowing how to get water to the point.

Most people have countless secrets behind their back, as a quick
    comparison
may reveal, but her secrets are not hidden behind. They are
between the flower and me. Right, she always carries her secrets in front
    of her.

金色秘密丛书

低头时，我只看见这菊花，
金色向导，小小的手臂曲张着，像软体动物的触须。
粗心看，才貌合成艳黄的花瓣。

而我现在心细得就像一根断弦。
养得这么好，一定懂政治，
于是，植物的礼貌就有了宇宙的深意。

一抬头，我瞥见了给它浇水的人。
她不是园丁，不过看起来她有更好的方法，
知道如何把水浇到点子上。

稍一比较，多数人的背后都有无数的秘密。
而她的秘密不在她身后，在我和菊花之间，
没错，她的秘密永远在她的前面。

2008.12

A BOOK SERIES ON MUSHROOMS

Pessimists rarely fall into mushrooms,
or remain loyal to the sensation they bring to you.
Common sense tells you, unless one betrays nothingness,
he won't be interested to find out the mushroom spirit:
they can do flips and rolls are better than human bodies.

They flip and roll in the pan, and flip and roll deep in your throat,
silky, tender, and not in the least afraid
of your snatching away what they have. Whatever truths
that optimists can think of, they will give them a form. They show
profound understanding, no matter what you try to hide.

They have smelt stewed chicks.
They welcome the contract between garlic and broccoli.
Their umbrellas open, falling and falling down into your heart,
and then turn into a nutritious little god.
Maybe, the difference between dissolution and digestion

is not as drastic as you think. Before dissolving,
one of them takes out a fresh menu,
asking you to devote more patience next time chewing on
the hints they offer. This world has not known any hint
that is closer to cosmic hint.

蘑菇丛书

悲观主义者很少会爱上蘑菇，
或像你那样，忠实于蘑菇带给你的感觉。
常识告诉你，没背叛过虚无的人
不会有兴趣了解蘑菇的精神——
它们的翻滚，甚至比肉体做得还好。

它们翻滚在平底锅里，翻滚在你的喉舌深处。
柔滑，鲜嫩，丝毫也不惧怕你
会夺走它们的一切。凡乐观主义者能想到的真理，
它们都会给出一种形状。凡你想隐瞒的事，
它们都能给予最深切的谅解。

它们闻到了小鸡肉的味道。
它们喜爱大蒜和西兰花签下的合同。
它们撑开的伞降落着，降落着，直到在你心里
变成了一个营养丰富的小神。
消失和消化的区别也许

没有你想得那么大。在消失之前，
它们中的一个从里面递出一份新菜谱，
请求下一次你能更耐心地咀嚼
蘑菇身上的暗示。还从未有过一种暗示
比它们更接近宇宙的暗示。

2010.11

A BOOK SERIES ON CELERY CELLO

I make a cello

out of a celery. It may be the world's

sveltest cello. So fresh is its look,

and its emerald strings even-tempered,

like you are well composed when facing

the toughest situations in the universe because

you have plenty of clues.

When you play it, I believe, you are using

a pair of hands that no one has ever seen,

not I and not even Death.

芹菜的琴丛书

我用芹菜做了
一把琴，它也许是世界上
最瘦的琴。看上去同样很新鲜。
碧绿的琴弦，镇静如
你遇到了宇宙中最难的事情
但并不缺少线索。
弹奏它时，我确信
你有一双手，不仅我没见过，
死神也没见过。

2012

EPITAPH

The heart-tomb stands upside down in the volcano.

When the engine of white clouds flames out,

blue is more enchanting than pure time.

Maybe this is not merely a memory,

for when the cherry ripens, you also mature.

Even if this is not obvious at the moment, it does not matter.

With due efforts, what is left in language is nothing

but a noble insanity. Take yourself for example.

You've lived through so much sorrow, and if it were

someone else, they might have been killed a thousand times.

But the falling flowers around here run ahead of Time's eyesight:

it seems that you are the only one in this world who has killed sorrow.

墓志铭

心坟倒立在火山中。
白云的发动机熄火时，
蓝，比纯粹的时间还迷人。
这或许不止是一个记忆，
樱桃的成熟中有你的成熟。
一时看不出来，也没关系。
用了力，语言能留下的，无非是
一种高贵的疯狂。比如你，
经历了这么多悲哀，
换别人，也许早被杀死一千遍了。
而在附近，落花却先进于时间的眼光：
就好像这个世界上，你是唯一杀死过悲哀的人。

2014.6.21

A PRIMER TO SHORT POEMS

To marry with a summer ant,

as if the black of its body is

a hidden fortune, profound enough to undermine

any power you could imagine.

短诗入门

和一只夏天的蚂蚁结婚，
就好像它身上的黑
是一笔隐秘的财富，幽深得足以摧毁
你能想象到的任何权力。

2014.8.7

A PRIMER TO THE TWILIGHT IN THE NORTHERN SHAANXI

The yellowness of the yellow soil cuts the world

into halves. One half is above,

but it is uncertain when the other goes below.

You are caught in life, like a suture thread,

slowly pulled through it.

More than a landscape is the west in the northwest wind

that cuts history into halves as twilight gradually

swallows the quivering voice of a motor.

For an instant, the vast desert seems still there,

but the lone smoke, well, is determined by the way

you look at my shadow from a distance.

陕北的黄昏入门

黄土的黄，把世界分成两半。
一半在上面，另一半
什么时候在下面，并不确定。
你，夹在生活中间，
像一条慢慢抽动的，缝合线。
更风景的是，随着马达的
颤颤声渐渐被黄昏吞没，
西北风的西，把历史劈成了两半。
一瞬间，大漠仿佛还在，
而孤烟，则取决于从远处
你如何看待我的影子。

2015.1.12

A PRIMER TO MARVELOUS TRAPS

If only you were generously gifted

to understand this damned metaphor!

Love is like a marvelous trap.

I fall into it with a golden tiger.

It falls hard, one of the front legs apparently

fractured, but it can still walk about.

It paces in circles, its roars

enough to shake and cave in a deep grotto.

A trap is not a grotto, though. Its space is merely of that size,

and it won't take long for the frantic fumbling

to turn into angry clawing and scratching.

I heard more vibrant roars before,

but I failed to grasp their implications.

The roars resonant in this trap, although

unfamiliar, get the message across

the instant I heard them. Every trap has lied to Fate,

no exception, but strangely enough, I have not in the least

been hurt. Perhaps it is due to my small build.

However, my bold speculation is, if I am a louse

on the tiger, I dare to swear

that the next in line will be you and your lion.

美妙的陷阱入门

但愿你有足够的天赋
理解这该死的隐喻：
爱，犹如一个美妙的陷阱。
我和金黄的老虎一起掉了下去。
它摔得很重，一只前腿好像
有点骨折，但依然可以走动。
它转着圈，发出的吼声
足以震塌一座长长的岩洞。
但是陷阱不是岩洞。空间就那么大，
用不了多久，强劲的摸索
便演变成愤怒的抓扯。
我听过声音更大的吼叫，
但并不理解其中的含义，
而这陷阱中爆发的吼叫
对我是陌生的，但我却一下子
就听懂了它的意义。没有哪个陷阱
不曾对命运说谎。但是很奇怪，
我一点没受伤。也许这和我身材瘦小有关。
但是你若敢猜测，我是老虎身上的
虱子，我就敢发誓，
下一个轮到的，就是你和你的狮子。

2015.3

A PRIMER TO BEING IN HANOVER

The train pulls into the station, and the doors open,

with the early summer sunrays throwing themselves in from outside

like dazzling ropes. Being shut in for so long

seems to have been for this moment alone.

Intense light floods in, shapeless spoondrifts

almost surpass the sparks of thought,

and the surges in the heart respond and echo, overwhelming

the subtle pressure that your resonant German

puts on my loneliness. Yes, I do care

if there is a rope in the sunrays—

perhaps this is a secret prescription

for myself so I can stay sane and alert

in a foreign land like Germany.

Stepping out of the train door, the slope of time

begins to tilt towards reality; I could feel

another me being dragged up an embankment

as if by a rope you once used.

人在汉诺威入门

列车靠站，车门开启时
初夏的阳光像晃眼的绳子
从外面扔进来。封闭了那么久，
仿佛就为了这一刻。
强光涌入，无形的浪花
几乎要胜过思想的火花，
而心潮呼应着，漫过
爽朗的德语给我的孤独
造成的微妙的压力。没错，
我很在意阳光里有没有绳子——
或许，这只是我个人
在像德国这样的异地
保持清醒的一种秘方。
跨出车门，时间的坡度
开始沿现实倾斜；我能感觉到
另一个我像是被你用过的绳子
紧紧拽着，爬上了堤岸。

At the end of my sight, an enormous dragon,

like a darting train billowing black smoke,

entered the tunnel of memory.

A person, never been betrayed by a secret,

quietly perfects your contours in the dust

that has not yet settled down.

Dear Hannah, should I be grateful to such

an illusion: at the station, a girl who passed by

looked too much like you at twenty-one.

And I slowly closed my eyes of a thinker,

so that the balance of the universe is kept intact.

而视线的尽头，一条巨龙
像驰骋的列车一样
甩着黑烟，驶入记忆的隧道。
从未被秘密出卖过的人，
在尚未落定的尘埃中
悄悄完善着你的轮廓。
亲爱的汉娜，我是否应该感激
这样的错觉：车站上，
一个与我擦肩而过的女孩
长得太像二十一岁的你。
而我为了保持宇宙的平衡，
慢慢闭上了我的思想家的小眼睛。

2016.6

A PRIMER TO RE-READING PAUL CELAN

Celan was right. Emitted from the tender
summer leaves, the continuous screams
can shatter the shadows of the world.

Inside the soil, love and rain
are often muddled by the tentacles of memory,
just like a water-soaked whip which,

although fiercely lashed, cannot always
hit accurately the core
of trembling punishment.

Mortality has been abused;
every bloom is a static explosion,
and the edge of the screams,

awakened as an extraordinary object,
may not be all of you
but may be the very little of you.

重读保罗 · 策兰入门

策兰是对的。从夏天的
嫩叶里，持续发出的尖叫
能击碎世界的影子。

泥土以内，爱和雨
常常被记忆的触须弄混，
就像浸过水的皮鞭

用力虽猛，但也不是
每次都能准确地抽打在
颤动的惩罚的核心。

必死性已被滥用；
每一次绽放，都是静止的爆炸，
以及那尖叫的边缘，

被作为一个非凡的对象
来唤醒的，不一定是你的全部，
有可能是极少的你。

2016.6

THE STRAIT GATE BLOOMS, OR A BRIEF HISTORY OF ROSEMARY
— TO GAO CHUNLIN

A body needs an occasional detached life from the soul,

But even when they are inseparable,

Its scent may be sent, when blown hard,

Into those invisible fissures of time around you.

It is so sylphlike already but still it is barely

Initiated into such a too-insensitive world, and there is no

Strong willpower, the ethereal stuff will surely bully the whirling.

Fogs and clouds will prop the emptiness of life up in the air.

The last trace of sanity, left over before she went crazy,

Drove Ophelia to flail her arm

And shower the petals of newly picked rosemary

Upon the Prince of Demark. Doesn't this mean anything?

A request, accompanied by the incomparably beautiful fluttering

Of a butterfly, when carried by its wings, has become

As precise as the inhaled air that runs into the lungs.

If destiny cannot be named after love, what can it mean?

窄门开花，或迷迭香简史
——赠高春林

肉身和精魂需要偶尔分离一下
但无法分离的时候，
可以把它的香气使劲吹进
你身边那些看不见的时间的缝隙。

袅娜到这一步，其实也才
算刚刚入门，世界太麻木，
定力不够的话，缥缈就会欺负缭绕。
用云雾架空人生的虚无。

发疯前最后残留的一点理智
让奥菲利亚挥舞着手臂，
将新采的迷迭香花瓣撒向
那个丹麦王子，还不说明问题吗。

一个请求，伴随比蝴蝶的翅膀
还要美丽的扇动，经过它的传递
已精确得像呼吸涌入肺腑
如果不能因爱而名，命运还有何意义？

Perhaps the purest one in you is the one

It really wants to work hard on: at any time,

The memory of love prevails over the contamination

The shadow of death brings to life; luck is also crucial, though.

A slight deviation would lead the tantalized nerves

To degrade into a fit of midnight screams.

Your desolation, if inserted into the horsehead fiddle,

Would suddenly become scraggier than the eternal sorrow.

或许最纯粹的你，才是它
想下功夫的那个对象：任何时候，
爱的记忆都胜过死亡的阴影
对生命的污染，但是否走运也很关键

稍有偏差的话，受刺激的神经
便会堕落成一阵午夜的尖叫。
将它插入马头琴，你的惆怅
会突然变得比万古愁还要嶙峋。

2018.7

2019.12

A PRIMER TO DEMOCRITUS

As the youngest son in the family, he was unfairly
Favored, therefore he did not need to bother
To dissect a rabbit if death came with truth;
And he fed the disassembled rabbit
To the leopard because it was angry at the cage.

Everything was planned very empirically. After the leopard,
It was rumored, he proceeded to dissect a lion,
despite the outcries of his neighbors. So here is the conclusion—
In terms of courage, to compare the essence of life
To a running lion, to say the least, is not a lie.

Plato, unable to bear the sight of blood, once bawled
That his madness should be chastened with flames—
Because Plato believed happiness was not anywhere
Outside the soul, not even anywhere after death;
Therefore, at any time, the key is to be quick at simplicity.

德谟克利特入门

很受宠，家里最小的儿子，
所以假如死亡能带来真理
他就不必费神去解剖兔子；
接着，他用解体的兔子去喂
对笼子感到愤怒的豹子。

一切都计划得很经验。据传言，
在豹子之后，他不顾邻居的反对
还解剖过一头狮子。结论是
就勇气而言，将生命的本质比作
一头奔跑的狮子，至少没撒谎。

见不得血腥的柏拉图曾叫嚷，
要用火焰来惩罚他的疯狂——
因为他相信，幸福并不在心灵之外的
任何地方，甚至不在死后；
所以任何时候，迅猛于简朴都是秘诀。

He was brought into court, but as a defendant
Of thought, he was lucky. Hippocrates testified,
And at least the tortoise that freed itself from the hawk's beak
Agreed with his idea: in respect of fate,
There is no imperfect world, but only undelightful people.

In his twilight years, he employed the dazzling light
Of the Aegean Sea to blind your own eyes,
So that the greatest darkness in life could be
Like an eternal memory to absolutely seal up
The Mediterranean beauty he adored when he was young.

他被带进法庭，但作为思想的被告，
他是幸运的。希波克拉底作证，
至少从老鹰嘴里脱落的乌龟
赞成他的想法：就命运而言，
没有不完美的世界，只有不快乐的人。

到了晚年，他用爱琴海的强光
照瞎自己的双眼，以便
人生中最伟大的黑暗
能像永恒的记忆一样绝对地封存
他年轻时爱慕过的地中海美人。

2019.1.5

A PRIMER TO POSSIBLE SALVATION

Mystical retribution comes from below.

That's right. It can go even further—

For instance, during a walk through darkness among rising fog,

It's possible for every step to kick at a freshly fallen leave.

可能的救赎入门

神秘的回报来自下面。
没错。还可以再往下——
比如，在起雾的黑暗中走着，
每一步，都能踢到新的落叶。

2014.11

A PRIMER TO THE SWAN AS AN ISOLATED CASE

In the dance of life, there is a question mark, snow-white,

that fleshes out with its own body

into a visible statue; it's stainlessly immaculate

and much more, and even its reflection becomes

so beautiful that it makes you a little embarrassed.

Silver-grasses, withered and yellow now, delay

not a minute and buy up all the blues of time.

The wilderness comes late but it still

poses itself as a perfect convergence.

The river is icy blue, just like when you rarely

thought of the slow-flowing waves

as the most ideal pedestal

for the statue. No need to worry

about the effect after it's installed;

over and above the clarity, a moving pedestal

goes perfectly well with the snow-white breathing statue.

Before the swan were seen there,

grebes and wild ducks had also appeared,

but obviously that place was reserved for it.

Still requires an explanation? Noble memory stays

above your shoulders and trusts nothing but its instinct.

The closer you get to it, the more you want to hold it back,

as if you have suddenly found

you have something you should give back to it,

but the pretense is no longer grounded.

以天鹅为孤例入门

生命之舞中有一个雪白的问号
被它用自己的躯体
充实成可见的雕像；岂止是
真的一尘也不染，连倒影
都美得让你有点不好意思。
枯黄的荻草也没耽误一分钟，
时间的忧郁已被全部买断。
尽管已迟到，但旷野
依然是一次完美的收敛。
河水冰蓝，正如你以前
很少想过缓缓流动的波浪
其实也是极为理想的
雕像基座。安装的效果
完全不需要操心；
澄澈之上，移动的基座
正好配上会呼吸的雪白的雕像。
在天鹅出现在那里之前，
野鸭和鸬鹚也出现过，
但是很显然，那个位置是留给它的。
还需要解释吗？高贵的记忆
越过你的肩头，只信任它的本能。
离它越近，就越想叫住它，
就好像你突然发现
你有一件东西，应该还给它，
而借口已不成立。

2011.12
2014.3

A PRIMER TO THE SNOWMAN'S WORLD

Like us, it's just that the mystery of time
prefers pure birth; it, too, grows
from childhood to adulthood—
starting from a small pile of fresh snow
scooped up with both hands, after layers
of careful support and snow-white patting,
until it finally takes one more step forward,
before nightfall, than its outline
and quickly matures into a beautiful plump snowman.

Once you realize that, it's hard
to deny that a person's best sense of achievement
is white, just like the color of snow.
Through us, the creative impulse seems to have found
a new object of affection; the naïve silliness is always endearing,
otherwise, the suffering it endures will be worthless;
once you realize this,
you will know its appearance cannot be accidental.
Its comfort is profound, yet direct.

雪人世界入门

与我们一样，只是时间之谜
更偏爱纯粹的诞生；
它的成长，也是从小到大——
从最初用双手捧起的
一小堆新雪开始，经过层层
细心的扶持，雪白的拍打，
在天色暗下来之前，
终于比轮廓更进了一步，
它迅速丰满成一个漂亮的雪人。

一旦意识到那一点，
也就很难否认，人的最好的成就感
也和它的颜色一样，是雪白的。
通过我们，那造物的冲动
仿佛爱上了新的对象；憨态始终可掬，
否则所受的苦，就没有任何意义；
一旦感觉到这一点，
它的出现，就不可能是意外。
它的安慰很深奥，却也很直接。

However, sometimes you wonder

whether the snowman's world and ours

could be mistaken. There is on its body

a snow-white standard, which can be harsh at times.

If it truly is a snowman, then who are we?

If it merely cooperates with us passively

to achieve something,

this game, and this joy, cannot

touch and stir so much innocence.

If its nose could never breathe,

if its eyeballs could never move,

if its lips could never quiver,

if its heartbeat could never

displace the shadow of the world in your calmness,

we might not even be entitled,

in the unrevealed part of the story,

to touch the question of who we are, let alone

use a dull mirror to please the melting time.

只是有时，你会警觉
雪人的世界和我们的世界
会不会被弄错？在它身上
有一个雪白的标准，有时会很刺眼。
如果它真是雪人，我们又是谁？
如果它只是被动地配合我们
完成了一件事情，
这游戏，以及这快乐
就不可能触及那么多的天真。

如果它的鼻子从来就不会呼吸，
如果它的眼珠从来就不曾转动，
如果它的嘴唇从来就不会颤动，
如果它的心跳从未令
世界的影子在你的冷静中错位，
我们恐怕在剩下的故事里
我们连我们是谁
都没有资格去触碰；更不要说
用迟钝的镜子去讨好正在融化的时间。

2017.1
2018.12

A PRIMER TO JINGTING MOUNTAIN
— TO WU SHAODONG

The best journeys always seem to be associated

with a feeling of going upstream. An invisible wharf

becomes more and more vivid among densifying chirps of birds.

When the door opens, we get out of the car

like jumping out of a rocking boat.

For an instant, the sealed time is filled with

the humming of bees. With this jump,

the barrier created by a thousand years between us

softens into clear footprints; this jump also

reveals that the human heart has never been much different

from the poetic heart; the embrace of nature

has never been merely a motherly snuggling to nature;

once the two become never weary of each other, the friendship

of a dense jungle will remain young. This jump also

distinguishes between the far and the deep,

disclosing which is a unique remedy: once in view,

the emerald green is, at any moment, more punctual than the ethereal.

敬亭山入门

——赠吴少东

最好的旅行仿佛总和
逆水的感觉相关。无形的码头
逼真于鸟鸣越来越密集。
车门打开时，我们像是
从摇晃的船舱里跳出来的。
密封的时间刹那间充满了
蜜蜂的叮咛。这一跳，
一千年的时光制造的隔阂
柔软成清晰的鞋印；这一跳，
也跳出了人心和诗心其实
从来就差别不大；自然的环抱
绝不只是贴切于自然很母亲；
一旦进展到两不厌，密林的友谊
依然显得很年轻。这一跳，
也区分了悠悠和幽幽
哪一个更偏方：一旦入眼，
任何时候，翠绿都比缥缈更守时。

It is easy to look back, but the calmness of the water surface

originates from the insight that the truth of existence has never been

more complicated than the reflection of the bamboo forest.

Alternatively, a life that is deeper than water

is a way of misleading when the world is concerned.

Scaling the steps, the phoenix is no suspense.

The azaleas are so eye-catching, so I guess the true meaning

of "not worship the height of a mountain" is: if no immortals were

there, how could we have shed so much sweat?

回首很随意，但水面的平静
却源于存在的真相从来
就不比竹林的倒影更复杂。
要么就是，比水更深的生活
是对世界的一种误导。
拾阶而上，凤凰才不悬念呢。
因为杜鹃如此醒目，所以我猜想
山不在高的本意是：假如从未有过神仙，
我们怎么会流出这么多的汗。

2018.9.19

A BRIEF HISTORY OF DUST

This life led in the labyrinth has hampered

the flower of structuration by which

I cultivate new varieties. When couriers pass by,

the frequency of growls and woofs leads to

the inference that the tottering shadows may often

diffuse to form a northerly mood. And then,

as yellow butterflies fly over the roses,

many boundaries will be further unbound:

for example, ghosts are the mood of the mute,

and untruth is the mood of truth.

In this way, it's best for us to have at hand

a solid object to symmetrize the universe;

it is said, tons of dark matter are permeating

our bodies at any second, but I can barely

feel the existence of those fissures.

尘埃简史

迷宫里的人生，已影响到
我培育最新品种的
结构之花。快递员路过，
从狗叫的频率，可以推断出
晃动的人影常常弥漫成
一种北方的情绪。接着，
黄蝴蝶飞越蔷薇时，
很多界限会进一步松动：
比如，幽灵是哑巴的情绪，
不真实是真实的情绪。
如此，我们的身边最好能有
和宇宙对称的实物；
据说，每一秒种都有成吨的暗物质
穿越我们的身体。而我几乎
感受不到那些缝隙的存在。

To avoid fear, the maximum trueness

appears unable to bypass our interstellar travelers,

who most probably have been sieved out

and have temporarily blocked the fissures.

Read the history of dust. It is greyish dust

that makes the blind language for life.

You'd feel whether your fingers still need to save

some tenderness for the red leaves in the Yan Mountains,

even though you were not conscious enough then,

and you like to boast that from the dust we come

and to the dust we return. But the fact is,

dust is never there to provide a convenient exit.

It did bury the faces of people, but the dust is

only the mood of the universe; and they are still diffusing;

dust will carry you and me along, and in a wondrous

strangeness, the journey continues.

想避免恐惧的话，最大的真实
仿佛已绕不过我们很可能是
已被过滤的，并且暂时堵住了
那些缝隙的星际旅行者。
读一读尘埃史吧。灰蒙蒙的
尘埃才是生命的盲文。
感觉一下你的手指是否还为
燕山的红叶保留着必要的温柔；
即使你那时并不知情，
喜欢自诩我们来自尘埃，
也将归于尘埃。但其实，
尘埃并不是用来解脱的。
掩埋过人的面目，尘埃是
宇宙的情绪；而且它们仍在弥漫；
尘埃会带着你我在奇妙的
陌生中继续它们的旅行。

2019.9.25
2021.3.3

A BRIEF HISTORY OF BEECHES

After entering winter, those egg-shaped leaves

in their endless falling participate in a remote divination,

but the results are somewhat ambiguous;

if it were not for the location,

which has been unnoticeably marked since spring,

it would be still impossible, even though

the howling of the north wind has already known

that some of your moods should be given care,

for you to recognize them instantly

only by their bare branches. To highlight their figure

from their murky fate requires you to provide birthmarks

with entirely different stories. Yes, these marks

should have been left by squirrels in their nervous skips.

Your stomach is borrowed so that when invisible hunger

becomes increasingly dangerous, there are still

bitter tree seeds in the world's stomach

being slowly digested into the metabolism of language;

after energy conversion, those marks of skips

will deepen your gaze, and your memory will go with

the memory of winter and gets a sublimation—

even though you may not necessarily need it.

榉树简史

进入冬天后，那些卵状树叶
在无尽的飘零中参与了
偏僻的占卜，但效果却有点暧昧；
如果不是所在的位置
从春天起就被悄悄做过记号，
即便北风的呼啸已知道
你的有些情绪应该得到特殊的照顾，
你也不可能仅凭光秃秃的枝条
就能立刻认出它们。将它们的身姿
从晦暗的命运中突显出来，
需要你提供完全不同的
故事的胎记。没错，这些痕迹
应该就是松鼠在紧张的跳跃中留下的。
你的胃被借用，以便看不见的饥饿
变得越来越危险时，世界的胃里
可以有那些微苦的树籽
被慢慢消化成语言的新陈代谢；
能量转化后，那些跳跃的痕迹
会加深你的凝视，而你的记忆
会伴随着冬天的记忆，获得一次升华 ——
虽然你不一定会需要它。

2015.12
2021.4

A BRIEF HISTORY OF AMBER-COLORED RITUAL

The amber-colored bottle
works best.

Under what circumstances, would a butterfly give up
its power to flutter and allow the tropical shadows
to glide into the backdrop of life?

When the suspense of the sea is surveyed,
the rare heatwave tinges our silence.
The reefs are like broken fingers, the color of death,
unknowingly, has been replaced by a faithful dark brown;

the long sleep of a beetle can then
be compared to a perfect piece of art;
it even has a frozen heart of aspiration, more eye-catching
than the sudden appearance of a small protagonist,
completely transparent in your randomness
that has been disrupted by pre-historic time.

琥珀色仪式简史

琥珀色的瓶子
效果最好。

什么情况下，蝴蝶会放弃
煽动的权力，听凭热带的阴影
滑向生活的背景？

比较过大海的悬念，
罕见的热浪润色我们的沉默。
礁石如断指，死亡的颜色，
不知不觉，已被忠实的深棕色替代；

一只甲虫的长眠
因而堪比一件完美的艺术；
它甚至有一颗已凝固的野心，
比突然出现的小主角
还醒目，完全透明在你的已被史前时间
打乱了的偶然性中。

The trance of life may well be

a radicalness of fate.

Thus, I never underestimate the trance of white clouds.

For example, I unscrew the bottle

and pour all the sadness into it;

after I gently screw the cap tight, the result is remarkable,

as if the entire constellation of Sirius disappears

in a circular stillness.

人生的恍惚未必就不是
一种命运的激进。
如此，我从不低估白云的恍惚。

又譬如，我拧开瓶子，
将全部的悲哀装入瓶中；
轻轻拧紧瓶盖后，效果显著得就好像
整个天狼星座也随即消失在
一个圆形的静止中。

2018.9

2019.2

A BRIEF HISTORY OF INSECTICIDE

Sealed in two small elegantly shaped cans

with signs of killing printed on them,

they nestle in the corner. They are persistently

quiet ever since bought home, barely

moved. Even during household cleanups,

their bases seem welded in and have never

been moved. Perhaps a little neglected,

but not ignored. Still in sight,

only the thick layer of dust settling on it

sometimes makes the laziness of life

differ from the conflicts in life.

It is obvious that if they are frequently used,

there will not be so much dust now

trying to permeate this poem,

seeking answers to mysteries. It's better to know,

when popular aesthetics of poetry is concerned, a poem

about insecticides, if implying some special answer,

should refrain itself from mystery. Maybe,

it can be traced back: they were originally

杀虫剂简史

装在印有杀戮暗示
外形精美的两个小铁罐里，
依偎在墙角；买回家后，
它们一直很安静，摆放的位置
几乎没有移动过。即使大扫除时，
它们的底座也像焊死了似的，
没有挪动过。或许有点被冷落，
但谈不上被忽略。仍处于
视线之内，只是上面落着的
厚厚的灰尘，偶尔会让
生活的懒散有别于生活的矛盾。
事情很明显，如果经常使用的话，
此刻，就不会有那么多灰尘
试图渗透到这首诗中
寻找神秘的答案。要知道

used to deal with the moth flies in flowerpots,

but as new cracks suddenly strike

the master's worldview, the purpose of their use

has also changed quietly; expired for a long time,

the toxicity must have been lost completely; another use

slowly shows: quietly stacked there,

they appear to be the props of kindness.

Only the dust faintly remembers the master's decision:

to use toxaphene and organochlorine to kill

the tiny insects that flutter among green leaves

appears to be an unsolvable moral dilemma.

To borrow from Aristotle, the dust

Is already a catharsis, which is higher than death.

按流行的诗歌美学，一首写杀虫剂的诗
假如包含有特别的答案，
是不该沾边神秘的。或许
可以这样溯源：它们原本
是用来对付花盆里的毛蟓的，
但由于主人的世界观突然
发生了新的裂痕，它们的用途
也悄悄改变了；已过期很久，
毒性想必已彻底失效；另一种作用
正慢慢显露出来：静静地存放那里，
就近乎仁慈的最小的道具。
只有那些灰尘隐约记得主人的决定：
用毒杀芬和有机氯杀死
那些飞舞在绿叶间的小昆虫
仿佛遇到了一个无解的道德难题。
如果可以引用亚里士多德的话，
那些灰尘，已是高于死亡的净化。

2020.4

2021.6

A BRIEF HISTORY OF HEARING AIDS
— AFTER ANTON CHEKHOV

Wearing it, you can hear the winter moon,

like the soles of a giant beast

stepping on the undercurrent of time

covered with black ice. When the direction

is determined, the soft strip-like echoes,

as if seals are torn away, constantly reveal

that between heaven and hell

there are irregular landforms

in an unusually active period.

One of the signs: after the primordial fear

appears, sharp stones are struck

by unknown objects more and more frequently;

but the most beautiful hand is also created.

Surely, you're not the only one having heard it.

After the scope of exploration expands,

butterflies reserve in the hidden wriggling

the exit to the spring in the cracks of the soil.

Unless the regulations for tests

助听器简史
——仿契诃夫

戴上它，你能听到
冬天的月亮，像巨兽的脚掌
踩过结着黑冰的
时间的暗流。方向
确定后，柔软的，
细条般的回音，像撕掉的封条
不断暴露天堂和地狱之间
有很多不规则的地貌
正处于异常的活跃期。

标志之一：原始的恐惧滋生后，
锋利的石头被不明物体
敲击的次数越来越频繁；
但最美的手，因此也被发明。
而且肯定不止你一个人听见了。
摸索的范围扩大后，
隐秘的蠕动中，蝴蝶
已在泥土的缝隙里预订好
春天的出口。除非彻底改变

are completely changed, the magpies

will always fail in their love calls.

Water needs to be replenished in time;

for extended attention span

is both a wonderful consumption

and a candid stake. If the free running

in the distance has not been replaced,

you can even hear: your breathing is

gushing out from the horse's nostrils,

slowly shielding all the background sounds.

测试的规制，否则
喜鹊的叫声在爱的呼唤中
一直会不及格。水分需及时补充；
以便持续的专注，既是美妙的消耗，
也是豁然的赌注。如果远处
那自由的奔跑不曾被顶包，
你甚至能听见：你的呼吸
正从马的鼻孔里喷薄而出，
慢慢覆盖了所有的背景音。

2022.2

A BRIEF HISTORY OF A JULY BRIDGE

Take off your shoes, expose your bare feet, twice a day.
In the morning, one-way and downwind, with occasional startling bells;
behind you lies the only thing not to worry about:
The sweating dawn light has pierced the bullseye of the world.

The time at night includes at least
two trips, hurrying back and forth. In the interlaced view,
mandarin ducks have no time for playing in the water;
that's a misleading implication, like lamentation is no longer corrosion-
proof.

No news is the best news --
this arc is perfect, no less than the rainbow after a thunderstorm
that splits you into two worlds: the heart is steep,
but because of the symmetry, the starry sky is flat.

七月桥简史

脱鞋，露出赤脚，每天经过两次。
早上，单向且顺风，偶有车铃惊悚；
在你身后，唯一不需要担心的，
出汗的曙光已将世界的靶心穿透。

晚上的那次，至少包括
两个匆忙的来回。交错的视野里，
鸳鸯才没功夫戏水呢；
那是错误的暗示，如同哀怨已不防腐。

没有消息就是最好的消息——
这弧度很完美，不亚于雷雨后
彩虹将你分身在两个世界：内心很陡峭，
但因为有对称，星空很平坦。

2015.7
2022.8

A BRIEF HISTORY OF PURPLE ADVICE

In wartime, oak barrels are good

for two things only: booze or booty.

Half of the booze is beauties and floating clouds

that finally break free from respective

prototypes. Time is limited;

can you see clearly? All the vortexes

come from the loins of grapes;

or, richness put aside,

those facial expressions can also come

from the floating clouds with curls at heart. As for the booty,

the question of whether it looks like a country can be ruled out.

After knocking, its empty inside is like a rabbit hole

that has been entrenched with countless snake shadows

gentler than illusions. After peeling, it is found

the cup is not the selected color;

if it is not properly controlled, emotions can be easily

turned to the ribs of the Milky Way;

but now, the treetops are shallower than a nap,

the sun is too scorching; as a non-mainstream project,

to chase clouds, or ride on the backs of geese,

is best done when the sunset is as red as a winning lottery ticket.

紫色的忠告简史

战争期间，橡木桶里
只适合装两种东西：酒，或赃物。
酒的一半，是美人和浮云
终于从各自的原型中
挣脱。时间很有限，
能看清楚吗？全部的旋涡
出自葡萄的腰肢；
或者，谈不上丰富不丰富，
那些表情竟然也可以
出自浮云很卷心。至于赃物
像不像江山，已可以排除。
敲击之后，里面空得像兔子洞里盘踞过
无数道比假象更温柔的
蛇影。剥皮之后，才发现
杯子的颜色没选好；
没控制好的话，很容易就导致
情绪像银河的肋骨；
但现在，树梢比午睡还浅，
阳光还太毒；作为非主流项目，
追云，或骑鹅旅行，
最好等到落日红得像中奖彩票。

2022.8

A BRIEF HISTORY OF SUMMER-DAY METHODOLOGY

There are methods. Peel a layer

of skin from self or shadow,

revealing the green inside, or purple;

but do not tap into whether the sacred mask

have not been damaged.

Once there is no need to match up,

just quietly dance along the blue of the butterfly,

join the song of shadows,

and play it to the secrets of the world;

thus, even the second-rate Death, nicknamed the Deaf, is also present.

So, even if the world

is truly not centered around the best of you and me,

it won't be too embarrassing;

the gaze from the peony is just fine;

if the gaze from the hydrangeas is added, it's more than perfect.

夏日的方法论简史

办法是有的。把自我或阴影
各削去一层皮，
露出里面的绿色，或紫色；
但不涉及神圣的面具
有没有被破坏。

一旦不需要对号入座，
就悄悄沿蝴蝶的蓝色舞蹈，
加入阴影之歌
对世界的秘密的播放；
这样，绰号叫聋子的二流死神，也有了。

这样，即便世界
真的不以最好的你我为中心，
也不至于太尴尬；
来自芍药的目光，就挺好；
再加上来自绣球花的目光，就更完美了。

2022.7

A BRIEF HISTORY OF THE CHAMBER OF SECRETS
— AFTER FYODOR DOSTOYEVSKY

After the rainstorm, the moving maze
Follows the washed traces and
Exposes it to the incoherent memory;
The seeped water is always a suspense.

There, the mystery of colors in the darkness
Continuously extracts, from the depths
Of the burning mind, a highly tactile paint
That looks comparable only to cooled magma.

There, the sufferers are their own golden bell;
The resilience ambushed in the muscles
Causes trembles that drive the stagnant time
Repeatedly into the adverse white night.

There, the closure will magnify every breath
Into the echoes of fate, and narrowness
Is not only a reality, but also allows
The accidental song to turn to the worship of shadows.

Up and down are just superficial opposites.
After going deep, the real boundaries come from the fact
That even if the abyss of the world has been measured,
It does not mean we can also find its entrance again.

密室简史
——仿陀思妥耶夫斯基

暴雨过后，移动的迷宫
顺着冲刷过的痕迹，
将它暴露在不连贯的记忆中；
渗下去的水，永远都是一个悬念。

那里，黑暗中的颜色之谜
从燃烧的脑海深处，不断提取
一种触感强烈的涂料，看上去
只有冷却过的岩浆才可与之媲美。

那里，受苦的人是他自己的金钟；
埋伏在肌肉中的弹性
构成的震颤，将静止的时光
一次又一次，驱动成对立的白夜。

那里，封闭性会将每一阵呼吸
都放大成命运的回声，
并且狭窄不止是一种现实，
也可让偶然之歌流向影子的崇拜。

上和下，只是表面的对立。
深入之后，真正的界限来自
即使丈量过世界的深渊，也不代表
我们还能重新找到它的入口。

2021.11.29

图书在版编目（CIP）数据

臧棣诗歌英译选：汉英对照 / 杨四平主编. -- 上
海：上海文化出版社，2023.6
（当代汉诗英译丛书）
ISBN 978-7-5535-2746-8

Ⅰ.①臧… Ⅱ.①杨… Ⅲ.①诗集－中国－当代－汉、英 Ⅳ.
①I227

中国国家版本馆CIP数据核字(2023)第080781号

出 版 人：姜逸青
责任编辑：黄慧鸣　张　彦
装帧设计：王　伟

书　　名：臧棣诗歌英译选

作　　者：杨四平

出　　版：上海世纪出版集团　上海文化出版社

地　　址：上海市闵行区号景路159弄A座三楼 201101

发　　行：上海文艺出版社发行中心

　　　　　上海市闵行区号景路159弄A座二楼 201101 www.ewen.co

印　　刷：苏州市越洋印刷有限公司

开　　本：889×1194 1/32

印　　张：5

印　　次：2023年6月第一版 2023年6月第一次印刷

书　　号：ISBN 978-7-5535-2746-8/I.1056

定　　价：48.00元

告 读 者：如发现本书有质量问题请与印刷厂质量科联系 T: C512-68180628